D1414750

To

....,

HAPPY BIRTHDAY

From

....

..............................., which piñata has the candy inside?

Shake the book really fast....

Come on, ...,
let's **POP** the balloons.

Ready?
Set?
Go!

Press here

HA, HA, ..., it's upside down!

Turn the book to see who's monkeying around.

Ready for your big present, ...?

Happy Birthday,
........................!
Now take a big
breath in and
BLOW
out your candles.

3, 2, 1...

HAPPY BIRTHDAY

MY FAVORITE PARTY GAME IS:

HAPPY BIRTHDAY

Draw your cake

MY AMAZING PARTY GUESTS ARE:

Illustrated by Hazel Quintanilla
Designed by Nicky Scott

Copyright © Bidu Bidu Books Ltd 2022

Put Me In The Story is a
registered trademark of Sourcebooks.
All rights reserved.

Published by Put Me In The Story,
a publication of Sourcebooks.
P.O. Box 4410, Naperville, Illinois 60567-4410
(630) 961-3900
www.putmeinthestory.com

Date of Production: May 2022
Run Number: 5025944
Printed and bound in China (LPG)
10 9 8 7 6 5 4 3 2 1

put me
in the story®
Bestselling books starring your child!
www.putmeinthestory.com